This book belongs to

_____

For Mia and our new baby
C. A.

This edition published by Parragon Books Ltd in 2014 and distributed by

Parragon Inc.
440 Park Avenue South, 13th Floor
New York, NY 10016
www.parragon.com

Text and Illustrations © Claire Alexander 2013

ISBN 978-1-4723-3185-4

Printed in China

That's When I Knew
A Big Sister's Tale

Claire Alexander

PaRragon

Bath • New York • Cologne • Melbourne • Delhi
Hong Kong • Shenzhen • Singapore • Amsterdam

My name is Poppy, and I am the smallest bunny in my family.

Everyone called me Baby until ...

... one day Mommy and Daddy brought home **a new baby.**

"Look at his big bright eyes," said Daddy.
"And his little fluffy ears," said Mommy.
"And his tiny paws," giggled Benji and Rose.
Everyone thought he was amazing.

But I wasn't sure.

The new baby
just slept and ate,
and when I said "Hello,"
he blew a raspberry at me.
That's not so nice.

"He IS only a baby," Mommy said.
"You'll soon be friends!"

So that night, I thought
I'd give him another chance.
I crept over to his crib ...

I looked at him, and he looked at me.
But then he opened his mouth and cried.

The new baby cried so loud,
he woke Mommy.

"Shh, little baby,
please don't cry," said Mommy.
And I don't know why,
but she walked him
up and down ... and up
and down.

But the new baby
cried even louder.

He cried so loud, he woke Daddy.

"Shh, little baby, please don't cry,"
said Daddy, and he bounced him on
his knee. (That always makes me laugh!)

Bouncy
whee!   Bouncy   whee!

But the new baby
cried even louder.

He cried so loud, he woke Benji and Rose.

"Shh, little baby," said Benji.
"Please don't cry," said Rose.
And they did their funny dance.

Hippity hop!   Hippity hop!

But the new baby
cried even louder.

I was about to tell Mommy
and Daddy they had better
take him back to where
they got him from ...

... when suddenly,
he looked at me
and I looked at him,

and he **stopped crying**
and reached out his arms.

The new baby felt SO small and SO warm,
and his heartbeat went

pum-pum
  pum-pum

pum-pum
  pum-pum.

Everyone was quiet, so quiet ...

he fell fast asleep!

And that's when I knew ...

...I love our new baby very much.